For Eleanor
—K. C.

For Juliet and Josephine
—J. M.

ATHENEUM BOOKS FOR YOUNG READERS

An imprint of Simon & Schuster Children's Publishing Division

1230 Avenue of the Americas, New York, New York 10020

Text copyright © 2018 by Keith Calabrese

Illustrations copyright © 2018 by Juana Medina

All rights reserved, including the right of reproduction in whole or in part in any form.

ATHENEUM BOOKS FOR YOUNG READERS is a registered trademark of Simon & Schuster, Inc. Atheneum logo is a trademark of Simon & Schuster, Inc.

For information about special discounts for bulk purchases, please contact Simon & Schuster Special Sales at 1-866-506-1949 or business@simonandschuster.com.

The Simon & Schuster Speakers Bureau can bring authors to your live event. For more information or to book an event, contact the Simon & Schuster Speakers Bureau at 1-866-248-3049 or visit our website at www.simonspeakers.com.

Book design by Ann Bobco

The text for this book was set in Museo.

The illustrations for this book were rendered digitally using Procreate.

Manufactured in China

0418 SCP

First Edition

10 9 8 7 6 5 4 3 2 1

Library of Congress Cataloging-in-Publication Data

Names: Calabrese, Keith, author. | Medina, Juana, 1980– illustrator.

Title: Lena's shoes are nervous : a first-day-of-school dilemma / by Keith Calabrese ; illustrated by Juana Medina.

Description: First edition. | New York : Atheneum Books for Young Readers, [2018] | Summary: Lena is excited about starting kindergarten but her favorite shoes are not until, with the help of her father and a very special headband, she convinces the shoes—and herself—to be brave.

Identifiers: LCCN 2017004123 | ISBN 9781534408944 (hardcover) | ISBN 9781534408951 (eBook)

Subjects: | CYAC: First day of school—Fiction. | Anxiety—Fiction. | Clothing and dress—Fiction.

Classification: LCC PZ7.1.C276 Len 2018 | DDC [E]—dc23

LC record available at https://lccn.loc.gov/2017004123

LENA'S SHOES ARE
nervous

a first-day-of-school dilemma

KEITH CALABRESE AND JUANA MEDINA

ATHENEUM BOOKS FOR YOUNG READERS

NEW YORK   LONDON   TORONTO   SYDNEY   NEW DELHI

Today is a big day. Today, Lena starts
kindergarten. Lena is very excited.

She has picked out all her favorite clothes to wear.

Her blue dress. Her pink striped socks. And her headband with the bright green flower.

There's just one problem. . . .

Lena's shoes are
nervous.

She looks for her dad.

"Oh, dear," her dad says. "What should we do?"

Lena doesn't know. She certainly doesn't want to miss kindergarten but she can't go without her favorite shoes.

This is a serious problem.

"Should we try talking to them?" her dad suggests.

Lena frowns. "We can't do that."

"Why not?"

"Because they're shoes," Lena says.

"Oh." Lena's dad thinks for a moment.

Lena thinks too.

"What about your other
clothes?" her dad asks.
"How are your socks feeling?"

Lena shrugs.

"The same as the shoes.
As usual."

Lena makes a face.
"Oh, no, they don't get along.
It's kind of a touchy subject."

Lena and her dad scratch their heads and look around her room. Then Lena remembers . . .

her headband.
Her headband with the bright green flower!
Of course. All her clothes like her headband.

"My headband is friends with everybody," Lena says.
"She could talk to my shoes."

"Excellent idea!"
Lena's dad says.

Lena places her headband beside her shoes.
She gives her dad a look.
"I'll just go wait in the kitchen," he says.

The shoes are shy and a
little embarrassed.

Lena encourages them
to use their words.

The shoes say
that school is big
and loud and different
and they'd really
rather not go.

The headband
is a good listener
and understands.

Then the headband reminds the shoes of other times they were all scared but decided to be brave, together.

And how things had pretty much worked out okay. Even better than okay sometimes.

(Because often the best things happen when we're nervous.)

Lena is optimistic. . . .

But the shoes aren't quite convinced yet,
and it's almost time to leave.

It seems Lena will have to go to kindergarten
without her favorite shoes.

"Oh, well,"
she says loudly,
so the shoes
will hear.

"Looks like
I'll have to wear . . .
my slippers."

Slippers?!

She wouldn't . . .

She couldn't . . .

She . . .

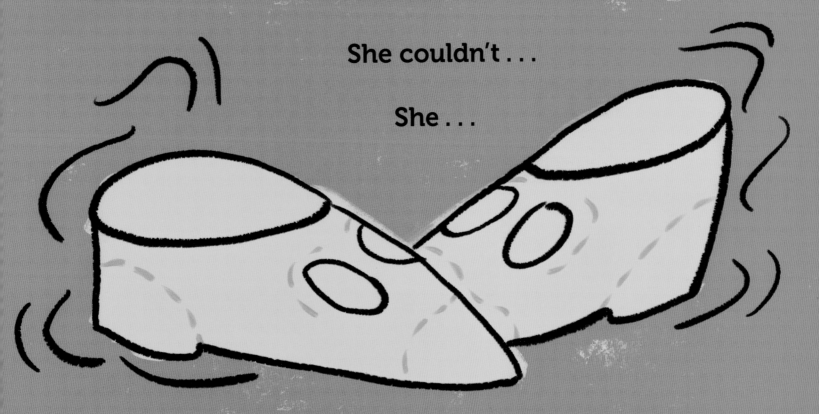

Her shoes confer urgently. And they decide . . .

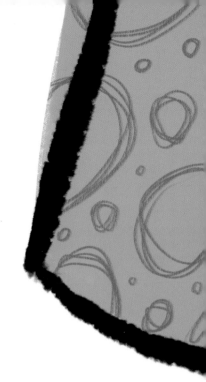

to be brave!
Lena is very proud of them.

Lena and her dad walk to school fo

he first day of kindergarten.

Lena's shoes get a little nervous again
when they step onto the playground,
and they make her walk
slower than usual.

But not for long.